To our friend Richard

First published 2015 by Walker Books Ltd, 87 Vauxhall Walk, London SE11 5HJ
2 4 6 8 10 9 7 5 3

This book has been set in WBHoráček
Printed in China

British Library Cataloguing in Publication Data:
a catalogue record for this book is available from the British Library
ISBN 978-1-4063-5828-5
www.walker.co.uk

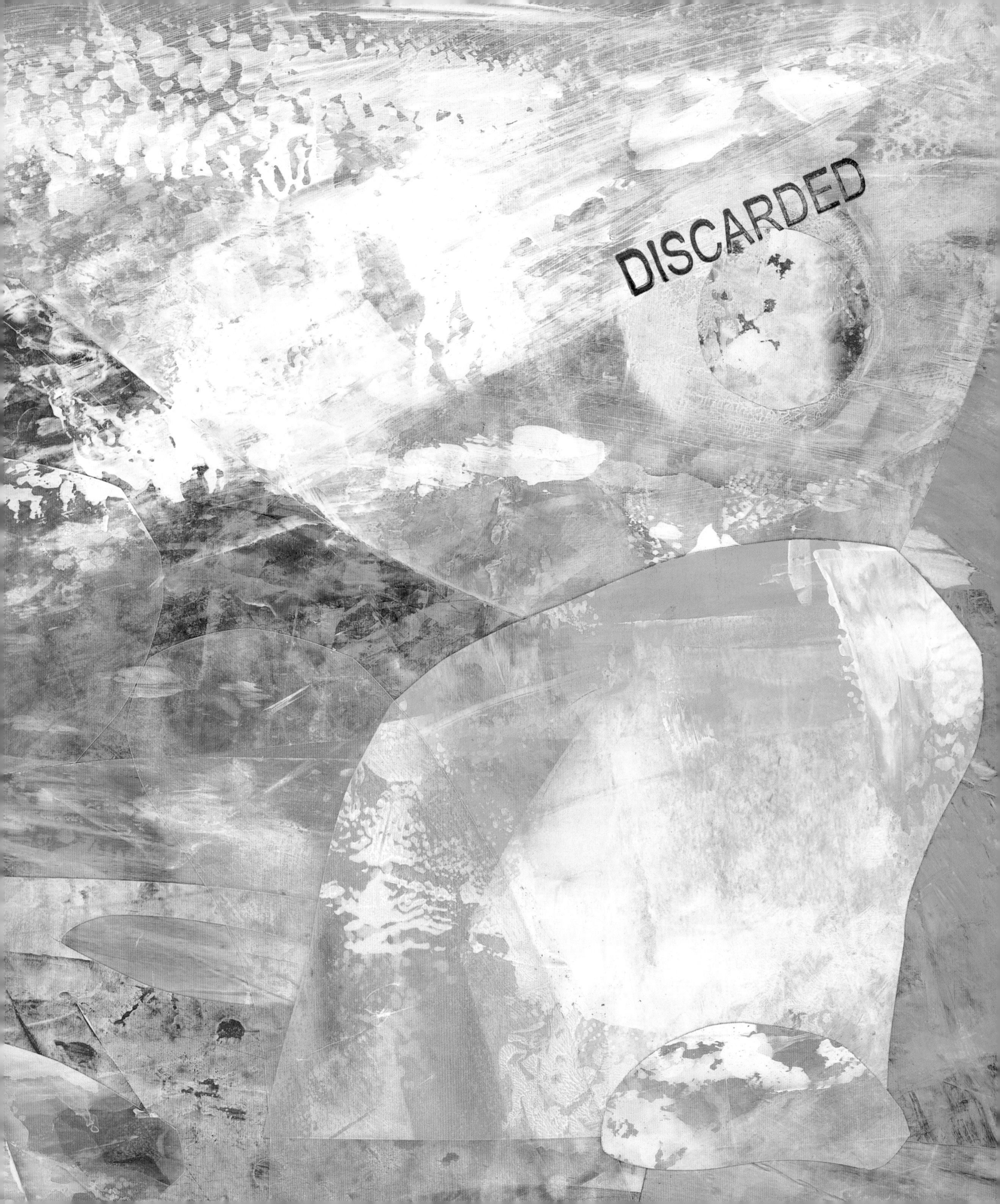

BLUE PENGUIN

Petr Horáček

WALKER BOOKS
AND SUBSIDIARIES
LONDON • BOSTON • SYDNEY • AUCKLAND

Far away in the south
a blue penguin was born.

A blue penguin is not
something you see every day.

"Are you a real penguin?"
asked the other penguins.
"I feel like a penguin," said Blue Penguin.

Blue Penguin
did all the same
things that the
other penguins
did.

He wasn't the best at
diving or jumping,

but he always caught a big fish.
“I told you I was a penguin,”
said Blue Penguin.

“But you’re not like us,”
said the other penguins
and they wandered away.

Blue Penguin was left all alone.
His days were filled with emptiness.

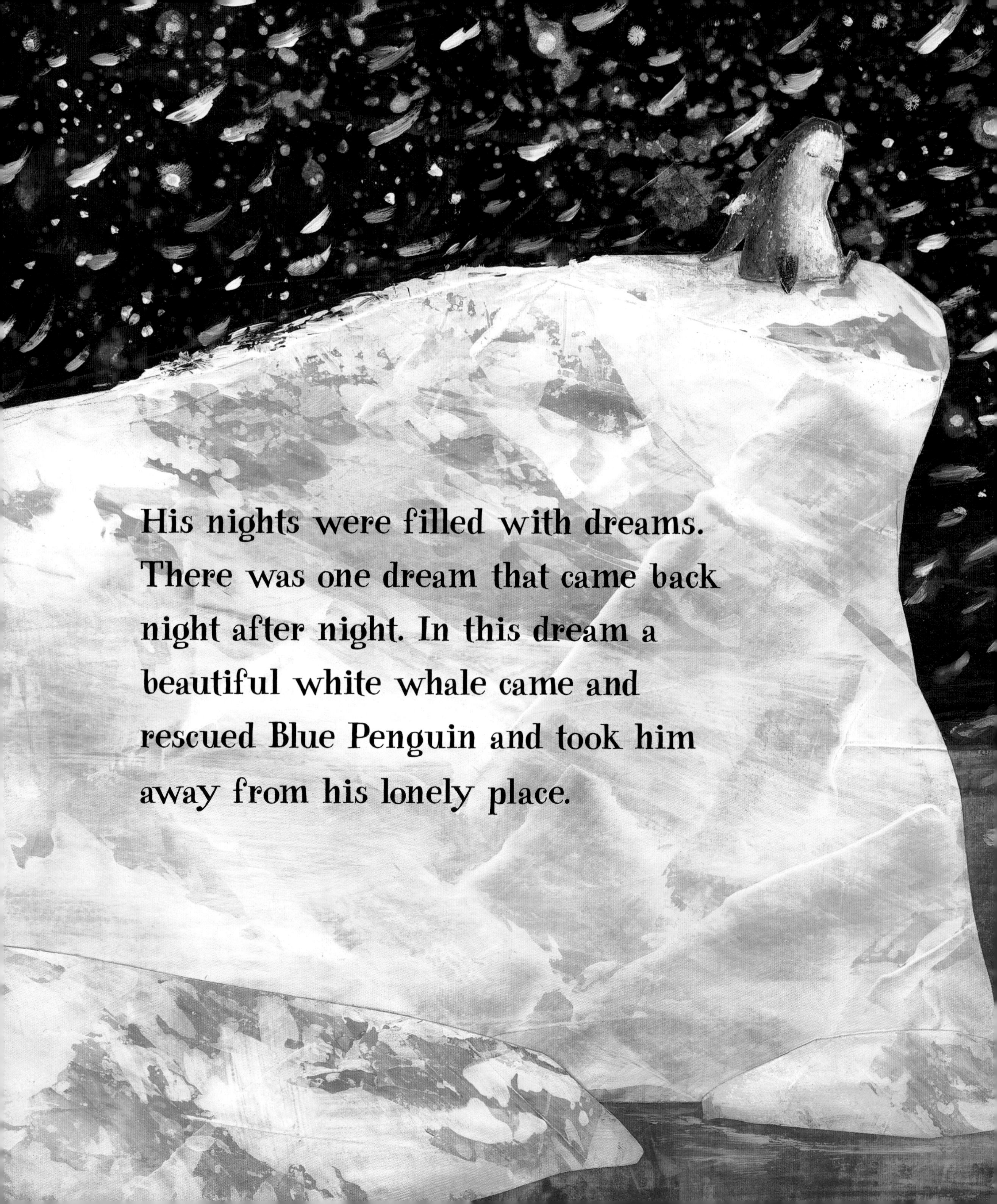

His nights were filled with dreams. There was one dream that came back night after night. In this dream a beautiful white whale came and rescued Blue Penguin and took him away from his lonely place.

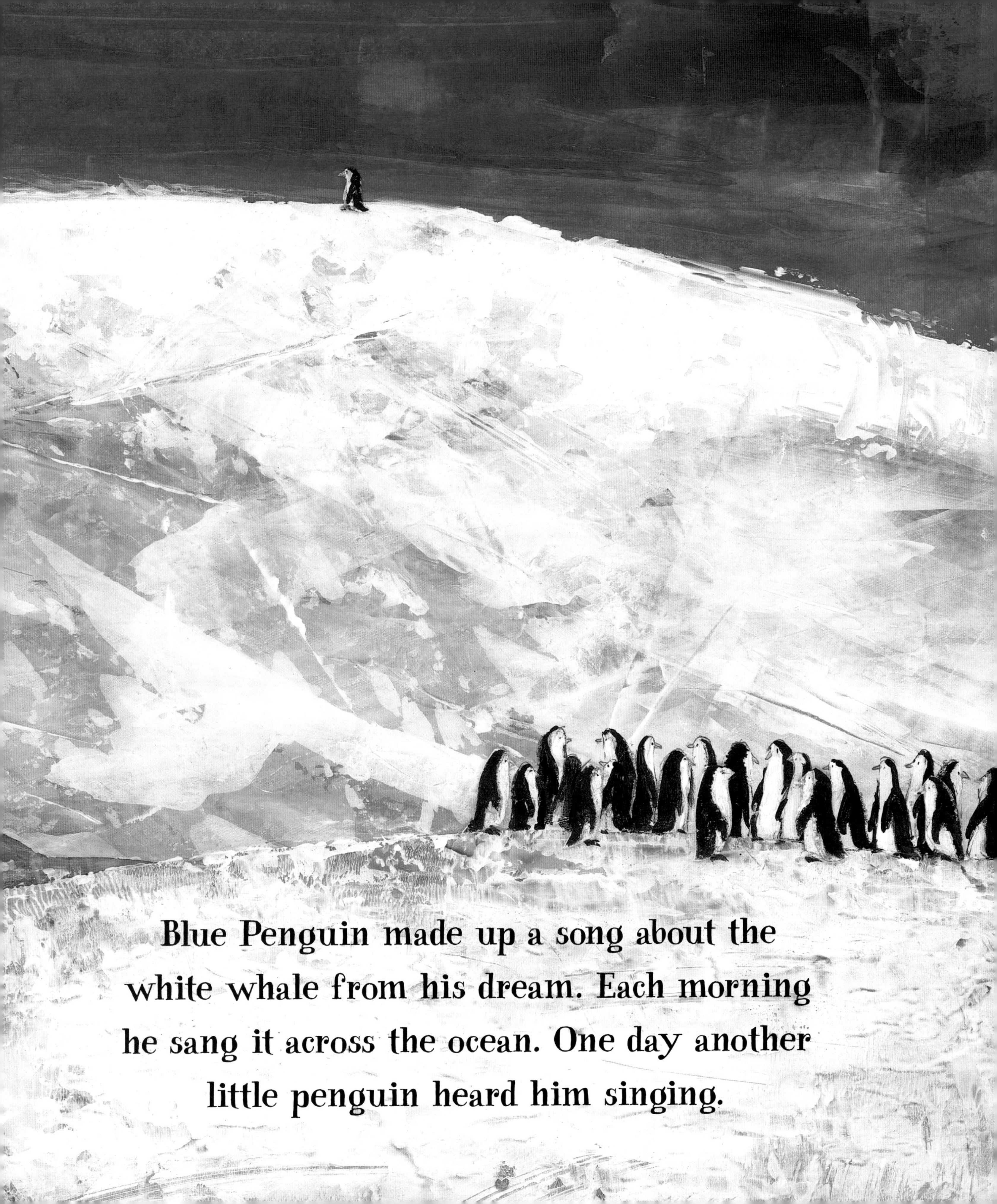

Blue Penguin made up a song about the white whale from his dream. Each morning he sang it across the ocean. One day another little penguin heard him singing.

Each day

she came a
little closer

to listen.

One day she spoke to Blue Penguin.
"Teach me your song," she said.

Each day Blue Penguin taught
Little Penguin a bit more of the song
and they sang and played together.
They became friends.

Then one evening Blue Penguin
spoke to Little Penguin.
"It's time we sang a new song,"
he said. "I will teach you."

Blue Penguin's new song was so magical
the other penguins came to listen.
When he had finished they came up to him.
"Your song is beautiful," they said.
"Will you teach us to sing too?"

"Yes," said Blue Penguin.
"Gather round and I will teach you."
But before they began to sing,
a huge white whale arrived.
"Who called me?" said the white whale.
"I heard my song and I have come."

Blue Penguin answered the white whale. "It was me who called you. I dreamed of you and wished you would come and take me away from my loneliness."

Little Penguin looked sad. "Don't leave us," she said. "You're my friend."

"Please don't leave us," said the other penguins. "We're sorry we left you alone. You're our friend as well. You're a penguin like us."

Then Blue Penguin looked at the white whale and said, “Thank you for coming for me, but the song you heard was a very old song. I have learned a new song now. I belong here.”

The white whale smiled, but said nothing. She turned round and slowly disappeared over the horizon.

Blue Penguin turned to his friends.
"Now let us sing our new song,"
he said. "Our song of friendship."